Waiting for Gregory

KIMBERLY WILLIS HOLT

paintings by GABI SWIATKOWSKA

Henry Holt and Company
New York

Henry Holt and Company, LLC
Publishers since 1866
175 Fifth Avenue
New York, New York 10010
www.henryholtchildrensbooks.com

Library of Congress Cataloging-in-Publication Data
Holt, Kimberly Willis.
Waiting for Gregory / Kimberly Willis Holt ; illustrated by Gabi Swiatkowska.—1st ed.
p.   cm.
Summary: A young girl eagerly awaits the birth of her baby cousin, while growing
more and more confused by the way her relatives answer her questions.
ISBN-13: 978-0-8050-7388-1
ISBN-10: 0-8050-7388-4
[1. Babies—Fiction. 2. Childbirth—Fiction. 3. Cousins—Fiction.]
I. Swiatkowska, Gabriela, ill. II. Title.
PZ7.H74023Wai 2006   [E]—dc22   2005012860

First Edition—2006 / Designed by Patrick Collins
The artist used gouache, watercolors, acrylics, enamel, and tempera on heavyweight,
hot-pressed Fabriano paper to create the illustrations for this book.
Printed in the United States of America on acid-free paper. ∞

10 9 8 7 6 5 4 3 2 1

For Shannon, who waited for
Mackenzie, Natalie, Gregory, Briley, and Alison
—K. W. H.

I would like to dedicate this book to Żak
and not to Seth Faergolzia of Dufus—
because Żak likes her very own space,
she might be willing to share it
with her dad, Mirek.
—G. S.

Aunt Athena is expecting a baby boy.
She says we'll call him Gregory.

"When will Gregory be here?" I ask Daddy.

"Soon, Iris," he says, "but not too soon."

"How long is that?" I ask.

"Oh, not too long," he answers.

"When will Gregory be here?"
I ask Grandpa.

"When the giant stork flies across the sky and drops
him over your aunt's house."

"Won't Gregory get hurt?"

"Nope. Your aunt and uncle will be waiting for him
with open arms."

I tell Grandma what Grandpa told me.
"Nonsense!" Grandma says. "He
shouldn't fill a little girl's head with
such silly tales."

"Then when *will* Gregory get here?"

"When the cabbage in your aunt's
garden grows large enough to make
soup for everyone in the family. She'll
pick that cabbage and there he'll be."

"Who?"

"Gregory."

"He'll be under the cabbage?" I ask.

"Exactly," says Grandma.

"Are you sure?"

"Absolutely," she says.

Only, *I'm* not so sure.

My friend Lacey claims she knows
when Gregory will be here, but it's a
secret. "I'll give you a hint, though.
Is your aunt's belly as big as last
year's first-prize jack-o'-lantern?"

"No," I tell her.
"Then it's not time yet.
Your aunt needs to eat a
thousand chocolate-chip
ice cream sundaes with
sour pickles on top."

I ask Mr. Conner. He's bound to know
because my mother says old people are wise.

"It takes nine long months to make a baby,"
he tells me.

"It does?"

"Yes indeed."

Finally, someone who knows something!

"You see, Iris," he adds, "you have to build
a ladder that will reach clear up to the clouds.
That's where all those babies live. It takes a
long time to build a ladder that tall."

I'm beginning to think Gregory will never
get here.

I tell Momma everything
I've learned. I tell her what
Daddy, Grandpa, and Grandma
said. I tell her what Lacey and
Mr. Conner told me, too.

"Oh, for goodness' sakes!"
Momma says.

"Are all of them right?" I ask.

"Well, every one of them is a little bit
right. Gregory will arrive soon but not too
soon. Babies do take nine months, but some of
that time has already passed.

"Aunt Athena's belly probably will grow as large as last year's first-prize jack-o'-lantern, although she won't have to eat a thousand chocolate-chip sundaes with sour pickles on top. When Gregory is born he'll be as big as a huge cabbage, maybe bigger. And you can be certain his parents will be waiting with open arms."

"But *when* will Gregory be here?"

"Do you mean the exact day and time?"

"Yes!"

"No one knows that," she says. "We will just have to wait and see."

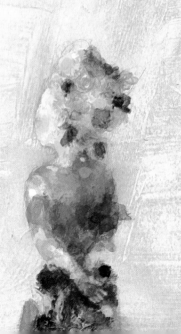

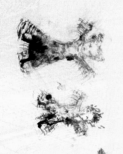

Every day I think about Gregory.
I want to show him how to make an
angel in the snow, but the last snowfall
melts and Gregory hasn't arrived.

I want to show him how to
make a wish with dandelions,

but the dandelions blow away
and Gregory still isn't here.

I want to show Gregory how to swim,

but summer vacation ends and the swimming
pool closes before Gregory is born.

Waiting for a baby is like waiting for a show
to begin.

Autumn arrives. The air turns crisp
and the first leaf falls from our apple tree.
My uncle calls!

"Guess what, Iris."

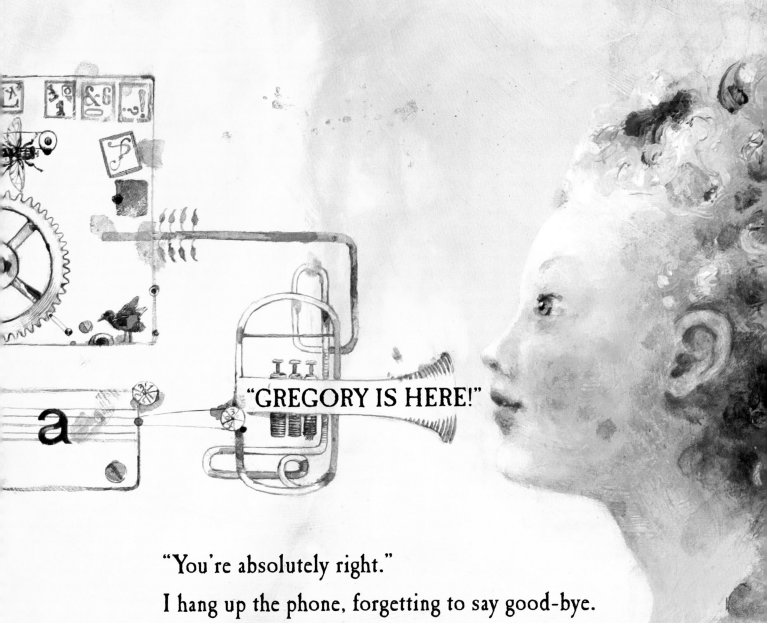

"GREGORY IS HERE!"

"You're absolutely right."

I hang up the phone, forgetting to say good-bye. I'm so excited I jump all the way to the kitchen and share the good news with Momma. I tell her everything that I'll teach Gregory.

"I'll teach him to fish,

a fish

to build the biggest snowman,

and to ride Grandma's pony.

I'll show him how to roll down the hill,

and
how
to
tie
his
shoes."

"Maybe we'll go see Gregory this weekend,"
Momma says.

Saturday is only a few days away, but it seems like
a very long time.

Finally, the weekend arrives and we visit Gregory.

He *is* bigger than a huge cabbage, but he's still very tiny, too tiny to fish, build a snowman, or ride a pony. Too small to roll down a hill or tie his shoes.

I'll have to wait for Gregory to
get older. Until then I can hold him,

push him in a stroller,

play peek-a-boo,

sing him my favorite songs.

He will grow and grow like a
wild sunflower.
And soon, but not too soon,
though not too long at all,
Gregory will be waiting for me.